Chapter 1

Jacob Daffren was a simple man. He cared not about riches, he cared not about fame. He was a family man through and through. While so many around were focused on rising to the top of society, Jacob seemed quite content with staying in the middle. He was older than most of the men working at the port. Whereas the median age was nineteen to twenty, Jacob was thirty. Did he gain respect with his age? Certainly not. The riff raffs and the scoundrels regarded him as a bother, not a superior. Perhaps it was appearance that was to blame. His skin was quite pale, his eyes were quite blue, and his frame was quite thin. Not exactly what one had in mind when they thought of an elder.

The year was 1901 and the Europeans continued to arrive in droves. The port of Ellis Island had been made the official landing for all immigrants coming to America from the east. It was *here* that this story begins. *Here*, where Jacob would witness something that would change the very fabric of his existence.

It begins on a Tuesday. The weather was rainy, the sky quite dark and the weather quite cool. Luckily, the Registry room was kept at a nice even temperature. Jacob sat looking forward towards a room full of people desperate for a chance to step onto American soil. It was his job to decide if they should be allowed, a decision he had to make in barely three minutes. He looked ahead at an elderly man that looked to be Japanese and waved him over. The man gratefully nodded and began to lug his large suitcase over to his line.

"Welcome to Ellis Island," Jacob smiled. "What brings you to America?"

The man looked to him with confusion and began to shake his head. He nervously reached into his pockets and pulled out a pile of folded up papers.

"Do you speak English?" Jacob questioned. The man shrugged and handed the papers over. Reaching for the crumpled mess, Jacob sighed, and began to unfold it.

"I need a translator," he abruptly called out. His voice rang throughout the room, summoning assistance in a rather hasty manner. A door on the far left side of the room squeaked open, and in walked a large fellow with a thick mustache, black hair, and a large gut. His steps were slow, his attitude quite lethargic and his demeanor quite unbecoming. Jacob looked in his direction and waved his hand eagerly into the air. The man nodded and proceeded towards him.

"What language does he speak," the man asked. His name was Henry and despite his unkempt appearance, he was actually rather young, no older than twenty-three Jacob thought.

"I'd guess Japanese."

Henry looked the elderly man over and shook his head.

"He's not even supposed to be at this port," he replied. He peered at the man with an almost personal contempt, then motioned him to step aside.

Jacob carefully handed the papers back to the gentleman, then began to browse over his list of names for the day.

"Anata wa Amerika ni nani o motarashimasu ka?" Henry asked. *What brings you to America?*

"Watashinoie wa moetsukite, watashi wa nani mo motteinai," the man replied. *My home burned down and I have nothing.*

Henry moaned and looked towards Jacob.

"He says his home is burned down and he needs a new place to live," he sighed. "Personally, I'd tell him this is the wrong port and send him out."

Jacob looked towards the man and glanced down towards the ledger at the name he had scribbled down. *Itoro Itcheman.* He glanced towards him once more, pondering as best he could the proper course of action.

"Tell him to proceed through the doors," Jacob replied. Henry looked aghast, as though he had just been told that he had to lick dog shit from the bottom of someone's shoe. The overblown expression would've seemed confusing, if one didn't know a bit about Henry. To say he was intolerant would be putting it lightly. For a man so versed in foreign languages he sure did seem to detest most of the immigrants that passed his eyeline. Unfortunately, he was hardly the only racists working in the immigration office. The job almost seemed to attract the type.

"Are you sure about that?" Henry questioned. "He's not our problem."

"He's not your problem," Jacob rebutted. "He's my problem and I am going to give him a chance."

Henry shrugged his shoulders and looked back towards the strange acting fellow.

"Doa o saki ni susumu," he sighed. *Go ahead through the doors.* The man smiled with an eager expression, and offered a subtle nod. He quickly picked up his suitcase and eyed a door labeled *Money Exchange*.

"You'll need this," Jacob called out. In his hands he held a landing card. The Japanese man peered at it with confusion.

"Anata wa kore ga hitsuyōdesu," Henry inserted. *You need this.* The man gratefully grabbed the card and moved towards the exit. As he disappeared from sight, Henry turned, sharing a vengeful glare with his optimistic coworker.

"You should not have let him through," he remarked.

"Oh piss off Henry." Jacob turned his attention forward and waved towards the next person in the line. With his coworkers focus now shifted elsewhere, Henry decided to move towards the exit. He kept his steps quiet and tried his best to as stealthy as he could. He had an agenda, one that would alter the very course of his life.

The door to the Money Exchange was a simple, if not boringly designed piece of architecture. It was unceremonious which was surprising considering what the door truly represented. It wasn't merely a door that lead to a place to convert one's money. There was so much more significance behind it. Acceptance. It was the physical embodiment of acceptance. To walk through it meant you had been allowed to stay, to join the American way. One would've expected a much more elaborate affair, but instead, it was nothing more than a dark stained door with a simple push handle.

Henry stepped inside and smiled as he gazed upon his intended mark. Walking just ahead of him, towards a long line, was the Japanese Man. With a smirk, he approached, moving past people from all different walks of life. For Henry, this place didn't feel like a melting pot of acceptance—no—it felt like a cesspool. A harbor for foreign disease and odors.

"Excuse me," he called out. Evidently, he had already forgotten the man's foreign nature. The man pressed forward and joined the line. Henry cautiously approached and tugged on the man's shoulder.

"Watashitachiha machigai o tsukutta." *We made a mistake.*

"Dōiu imidesu ka?" *What do you mean?*

"Anata wa kono minato ni shozoku shite imasen. Anata no kādo ga hitsuyōdesu," Henry replied. *You don't belong at this port. I'm going to need your card.*

Suddenly the man pulled back, looking at Henry with frustration. He waved his hand in the air and motioned for him to *go away*. Feeling an air of confidence, and perhaps a bit of unfounded authority, Henry reached towards the man's hand and retrieved the card.

"Nē!" The man declared. *Hey!* He looked towards the front of the room and began to wave his arm with haste. Stuffing the card into his pocket, Henry reached forward and gave the man a firm pull.

"I know you don't understand what I'm saying, but your race doesn't belong here. And I don't just mean at this port. I mean here. In our country," Henry whispered. He gave the man a tug and began to pull him towards another door. An exit. The Japanese man began to yell, kicking and squirming with protests. Soon all eyes were fixed on the display, and as the embarrassment began to add up, so too did Henry's anger. He wanted him out and he wanted the display to stop. He had hoped that being in his position, he would be taken a bit more seriously. Evidently, however, the man was far more stubborn than he had expected.

He gave the handle a quick twist while being sure to keep his grip securely tightened on the Japanese man. They were outside. A cold breeze blew through the air. A reminder that winter was just around the corner.

"Yameru Yameru!" The man hollered. *Stop Stop!* Planting his feet firmly against the stone ground, he locked his leg and gave his arm a firm tug. Henry's grip faded, and he stumbled forward. The Japanese man lifted his suitcase, swinging it towards Henry with as much strength as he could muster. The attack was effective. Henry fell, holding his head as a migraine began to spread.

Itoro promptly dropped his suitcase to the ground. It took all of thirty seconds for him to open the case. Inside, were his clothes and essentials, things that would've already been inspected. He reached into the case, towards a pair of brown dress shoes and reached his hand inside. He withdrew a small jar and held it up to his eyes. Inside appeared to be sand. Something was amiss though. The sand appeared to be in motion, almost as though it were alive. He opened the top, and climbed to his feet in time to be greeted by an angry expression from Henry.

"You're so fucking dead," Henry declared. He lunged forward, but at the same moment, Itoro flung the contents of the jar forward. A small amount landed on Henry's sleeve, and almost immediately, the material began to consume his clothing.

"What the hell?" He looked with horror as the strange, brown granules continued to make their way up his sleeve. Quickly, he pulled the coat off, tossing it to the ground.

Itoro looked towards Henry once more, and flung a bit more of the mysterious contents forward. A gust of wind suddenly blew. A northern wind with small traces of snow hiding on its frigid breath.

"Ahh!" Itoro roared. The gust had blown straight towards him, bringing the substance careening right back at him. The granules connected with his face, and began to quickly spread. He dropped the jar, falling to his knees in pain. What happened next left Henry shaken to the very core. The glass of the jar shattered, freeing the contents in a most unholy manner. Like a snake in the grass, the granules began to move towards him, slithering in a back and forth motion.

"Fuck this!" Henry exclaimed. He turned around and began to quickly head for higher ground. Ahead of him, Itoro continued to be consumed by the strange substance. The process didn't take long. After the granules had finished, they slowly moved their way down. Itoro had been utterly destroyed. His skin was eaten entirely away, replaced instead with a black mucus that slowly seeped down towards the ground. In his eyes, there was a faint trace of recognition. He looked onwards, towards Henry, who cowered with fear.

"Unmei wa anata no tame ni kuru," Itoro whispered. With that, he fell over.

"What the hell happened here?" An officer abruptly demanded. He stopped, and withdrew his revolver as he noticed the strange granules slithering towards the large rock that Henry had climbed atop.

"Shoot it!" Henry wailed. The officer took aim, firing a couple rounds towards the ground. The granules changed course. They headed towards the water line.

"We have to destroy it," Henry advised. He jumped down from the rock, and reached into his pocket. He eagerly pulled out a pack of matches and ripped one free. His hands trembled and his heart raced. The granules continued to maneuver towards the water line.

"Burn," he whispered. He scraped the match head against the striker, as the flame began to spread, he tossed it towards the granules. To their dismay the match erupted in flames like fire to gasoline. From within the flames, a loud screech emerged, and a face began to slowly emerge. Eyes as dark as a cavern and a mouth like that of a gorilla.

"What is this?" A voice suddenly croaked. Standing in the doorway, was Jacob. He looked down, towards the mummified remains and gasped.

"What the hell happened?"

The flames began to quell, leaving nothing but an awkward silence.

The Itch Man

By M.P. VanderLoon

Copyright © 2017 by M.P. VanderLoon
All rights reserved. No parts of this book may be reproduced or scanned in printed or electronic form without permission.
This book is a work of fiction. Names, characters and events are products of the author's imagination. Any resemblance to person's living or dead is coincidental.
Print on demand provided by Createspace and Ingram Spark

ISBN-13: 978-0-9975194-8-8

ISBN-10: 0-9975194-8-7

Chapter 2

An overcast of dark, fluffy clouds filled the sky, creating a suffocating effect and blocking out all light. The sun was powerless today. It was chilly, bits of snow slowly trickled down, landing on the ground only briefly before melting. The newspaper had talked of flurries and chilly winds. So far, that seemed an accurate prediction.

Jacob walked quietly down the streets as he tried his best to keep himself warm. Today was his day off. It was his first free day in over seven days, and yet, now he had no idea what to do with himself. The constant busyness of the port seemed more like life than whatever it was he did when he wasn't there. The roles had become reversed. At work was his life, the rest was just waiting to get back to work. This wasn't exactly the mindset he had hoped for, but with the busy flow of incoming ships, it's just how it felt. Still, he tried his best to do all the things a young single man should. When he wasn't working on cleaning his apartment, he would visit bars. They were the best place for social interactions. With any luck, he hoped he would eventually meet an honest woman.

The cold breeze had started to pick up. Visibility had started to diminish and each passing minute outside left his nose and ears feeling like foreign objects that had been tacked onto his face. It was time to get inside. Luckily, the small restaurant he was looking for was just a couple blocks ahead. *Billy's* was a regular spot for those who wanted a home cooked meal, but didn't have the talent to do it themselves. The quaint restaurant seemed regularly busy, but despite this, he never had to wait too long. Marci, a young woman whom he had attended school with, always made sure to get his order in as quick as possible.

As the sight of Billy's caught his eyes, he found himself grinning. *I hope she's working*, he thought. From the front door, emerged an older couple that were dressed as though they were dining at a far fancier restaurant. Date night. He smiled as he approached and held it open for them.

"Thank you, sir," the woman smirked. They stepped past, leaving a vacant door for him to step through. He peered into the restaurant and grinned as he noticed Marci carrying a couple plates to one of the front-most tables. He stepped inside and paused.

"Sit anywhere you like Jacob," an older hoarse, voiced woman shouted. He looked to her quietly then scanned the openings. It was slim pickings for sure, but towards the back there was a small table that seemed perfect. There were still dirty dishes on it, likely from the couple that just left he thought. He glanced towards Marci once again, then proceeded back towards it.

As he approached the table it became quite clear the previous occupants were rather sloppy. Under the table there was scraps of food and on each seat there were crumbs. He couldn't help but sigh with amusement though. Marci was here. It was always hard to feel sour when she was around. Pulling his sleeve down over his hand, he wiped the seat clear and sat down.

"Sorry about the mess," Marci announced. She approached with a pad in her hand and a disheveled look upon her face.

"It's been a madhouse tonight."

Jacob smiled. "It's ok. You know I'm not as picky as most."

"Frank was supposed to get this table cleaned. He must be in the back stealing scraps again," she explained.

He nodded as she began to pick up the scattered dishes that littered the table.

"I can help you," he offered. She looked to him and shook her head.

"No, customers aren't allowed in the kitchen," she replied. "I'll get this taken care of and I'll be right back."

She turned and quickly disappeared into a door in the backside of the bar area. He sighed and looked towards the table. Once again, he used his sleeves to push aside the left-over crumbs. A conversation towards the front of the restaurant suddenly grabbed his attention. From the sounds of it they were young. He lifted his head and began to scan the restaurant. There was a heavy-set man sitting at the bar, an older, grey-haired gentlemen sitting at a table in the middle, and finally a middle aged man with two children. He peered at them with a jealous smile. Family. If there was one thing missing from his life, it was that.

"Cute," he whispered to himself. Suddenly, something in the far window caught his eyes. A man. Strange in appearance and in movement. His skin looked terribly dry, his head—bald and his mouth seemed noticeably missing. He gulped as he anxiously gawked at the grotesque display. The strange man turned, stopping in the middle of the street and looked towards him.

"What the hell?" Jacob muttered. He jumped up, pushing around a few people whilst keeping his eyes trained forward. The man in the streets continued to stare. He didn't move, not even a twitch. He just stared. All around him, people continued to pass by, as though he wasn't really there at all. And yet, with each further step, Jacob could feel the sting of his gaze. He felt nude, like his clothes had been stripped away and he was standing on a stage being critiqued.

"Watch it man," A fellow restaurant patron bellowed. Jacob halted as he noticed he had spilled a grumpy-looking man's beverage.

"What in the hell's the matter with ya?"

Jacob shrugged off the man's complaint and looked back towards the street. The man was gone.

"What was that?" He whispered. A hand gently pressed onto his shoulder.

"Are you ok?" Marci questioned. She wore concern on her face as she looked at him, then down towards the pooling ale that was moving across the floor.

"Oh shoot," she exclaimed. Turning around, she dashed towards the kitchen area and disappeared behind the doors. Jacob continued to look out the window and towards the streets. His mind was a hostage of fear and curiosity. He had seen something unexplainable. It had looked like a man but there was also something very alien about him. And then there was that look. That look of recognition. Whoever it was, it seemed as though he knew him. With his fingers trembling and his skin a bit clammy, he moved towards the door and pushed through the exit.

~

Twenty minutes later he found himself sitting alone in his apartment looking at a mostly blank wall. There were a couple portraits of his parents and one of a tree with red leaves, besides that, it was an empty wall. He had lived here only a few months, and while that seemed long enough to have personalized the place a bit, he hadn't really felt the need. His parents–after all–were long predicting his failure and eventual return home. He resented the opinion, but evidently couldn't discount it either.

He sat in a still wooden chair cornered by his thoughts and curiosities. In his hand, he held a pipe. As he pressed the stem against his lips, he took a long hit, holding it in for a moment, and then expelling it. His mind raced to the man in the streets. To the look in his eyes. It seemed almost accusatory. *But who was it?* Jacob had–in general–considered himself to be a pretty docile person. He tried not to make enemies. Sure, he had disagreements. Especially with that fool Henry from the office, but besides that he was pretty kosher with most others.

"Wait a second," he paused. He took another hit of his pipe. The strange man's outfit. It had stood out. Obviously, the most noticeable thing about him was his horrendous appearance, but beyond that, his clothes were most bizarre. It wasn't an outfit one normally saw in the city. Or in this country for that matter. Robes of some kind. Dark brown with strange patterns that reminisced dragonflies.

"I've seen that outfit before," he realized. Jumping to his feet, he raced to a nearby desk and placed his pipe down atop its surface. To his left was a stack of folders. Documents regarding the incident that had happened a couple months back.

"Where is it?" He whispered. Page after page, he skimmed until finally he came upon a photograph of the man who had perished that day. The man looked just as he'd remembered. Black hair cut in a bowl, small lips and eyes, and finally the black robes with the dragonflies. *Itoro Itcheman*. That was his name.

By all accounts that was the most bizarre day of his life. Working at the port, he had seen many strange things, but nothing could quite compare to the strange sand that man had brought with him that day. Most troubling of all was the fact that he had missed it in his inspection. *What was he really planning on using it for?*

He glanced over the picture, studying every detail of the man's expression as best he could. As he further inspected it, the obviousness of the connection to the man in the streets grew. But instead of feeling closer to answers, he found himself feeling further than he had before.

Thump thump thump.

The knock on his door cut through the silence like a machete through weeds. He dropped the picture to the floor and turned to look at the doorway.

Thump thump thump.

Whoever it was, they were persistent.

"Who is it?" He called out. His heart felt as though it were in his throat. Images of the strange man from the streets crawled into this mind. It was all he could think about. All he could imagine. He felt certain his late night visitor was indeed the malevolent figure he had seen just barely an hour ago. His feet felt weighted as he cautiously approached the door.

"I'm just freaking myself out," he whispered. He pulled the door open. Standing there was Marci. She was wearing the same outfit from earlier and she looked positively whipped. Her cheeks had that red hue they always got when she was stressed and her hair was tossed around wildly.

"Hi," he sighed.

"Hey," she replied. "What's wrong? You look weird. And you left earlier without even saying goodbye."

The image of the strange man popped into his mind. Once again, he felt the same chill he had before. That stuck feeling of not being able to move or talk.

"I remembered I had something to take care of," he finally replied.

"What was it?" She questioned. He paused and looked to the floor.

"Something for work," he retorted.

She looked to him with a skeptical scowl, then pushed her way past him. His apartment was as disheveled as it was the last time she had stopped by. She looked around with concern. In the far corner of the room, was his bed. Next to that was a small table with a small lamp, and scattered all around it were piles of tobacco.

"You smoke too much," she remarked.

"Helps take the edge off," he winked. He approached the chair he had earlier occupied and motioned for her to take a seat. She paused as she looked towards him, then finally accepted the offer.

"Do you remember that guy I told you about at the port? The one that died," he whispered. She solemnly nodded. He had told her the story almost the very next day. It had mortified her, but not because someone had died. No — what was upsetting for her was the fact that to date, Henry had gone unpunished for his part in the accident. How could a man who so bluntly caused a confrontation, who had tried to revoke the card that Jacob had approved, still be employed. The whole thing just seemed inexcusable.

"Of course I do," she quipped. He looked down to the floor and sighed as he observed the intricate details of the wood grains. Each grain told a story. The tale of a life that began as nothing more than a small seed and through years and years, became a mammoth, a life as big as it gets. But then, like all trees, it was cut down, processed and sold to men. Men who all had their own tales to tell. What troubles pestered the man who laid this wood? What things had he seen?

"I think I saw him today," he replied. "At the restaurant."

She turned her head towards him and offered a sarcastic smile. Jacob had always been a reasonable man. A man that was a skeptic in the most obvious sense.

"That's impossible," she retorted. "He was buried. You saw him die."

Jacob peered at the desk, at the photo of the man in question. Even in black and white, his accusatory stare seemed bright. Like it was a flashlight pointed straight at his face. He winced and picked it up. Slowly, he turned and handed her the photo.

"I saw him," he restated. "But he didn't look the same. His skin looked cracked and his mouth was almost missing."

He turned his focus back to the table, and then reached towards a drawing he had sketched. A drawing of the man from the streets. He held it out in front of him for her to see.

"That's how he looked."

Marci studied it, feeling obviously uneasy with the whole story. Believable or not, she hadn't ever known Jacob to be a deceiver. He was one of the most honest, and intelligent men she had ever known, more so than herself in fact. It was this quality that first allowed them to become friends all those years ago.

"You saw something traumatic. I think your guilt is making you see things." She stood from the chair and approached. She shakenly set the photo back onto the table, then turned back towards him with folded hands. There was a slight tremble to them, but she tired her best not to let him notice. She had to be strong.

"You're not at fault for what happened. Henry is. So please, try to get past this guilt. Stop beating yourself up. Stop letting the past haunt you."

Jacob peered towards the window. Darkness had spread over the city. It was in hours like these when despair and misery came out of the shadows.

Soon, the social outcasts would scavenge the city, looking for whatever they could and sometimes even taking it by force.

"It's getting pretty late Marce. Perhaps you should just stay here," he remarked. She turned and looked towards the window and shrugged.

"I'll be fine."

She threw her arms around him. As he embraced the hug he couldn't help but take in the scent of her hair. It was pretty common for it to smell like whatever had been cooked the most in the kitchen. This time it was roasted turkey. He drew a deep breath as he continued to feel her warmth pressed up against him. In her back, he could almost feel her heartbeat. It was the first time in a long time that he felt truly connected to another person.

Eventually she pulled away and strolled confidently over to the door. She pulled it open and paused.

"You think it's just in my head huh?" Jacob questioned.

"Yes," she replied.

Chapter 3

Samantha was a bitch. An uncontrollable bitch with an ugly temper and an irritating voice. That was Henry's take anyways. To him, she was demanding and hardly worth all the effort he had to put into the relationship. Still though, day after day, argument after argument, he stayed. He stayed because it was familiar. He stayed because he felt safe when he was with her. She was a plain woman. Modest in her clothes and light on her makeup. Her auburn hair was cut short, almost like a boy, and her teeth had a space in between the front two. An imperfection he had once thought was cute. Now it just annoyed him.

She had been his one constant. His rock, the person who kept him grounded. Lately, he needed it more than ever. Since the incident at Ellis Island, he had been quite irritable and a tad bit irrational. Always he walked around throwing accusations against her for things he had done. It was a tedious cycle of back and forth banter but no matter how illogical he got, she stayed.

As Henry sat in his brown, lint covered chair, he quietly read over the local newspaper. Across from him was Samantha. She sat with a gentle expression as she read over a local gossip magazine. Sitting on a small, brown end table, was a cup of piping hot peppermint tea. Two teaspoons of sugar and a dash of cream.

Henry continued to scan the newspaper as he tried his best to tune out the noise in the streets below. Christmas was fast approaching and with it brought an urgency to the residents that came with an unfortunate amount of noise. Soon, droves of children would fill department stores as they searched for the latest and greatest in toys. He took a sip of his coffee and peered over his cup towards her. She seemed oblivious to his stare.

"Should we go look for something for your nephew?" He finally asked. She looked up from the magazine shocked.

"You want to go shopping?" She questioned.

"Not really. But I thought it seemed like a good idea to get a head start on the crowds."

She set the magazine down and looked to him with a bit of pride. He had always displayed a clear lack of interest in her family. It was a welcome, if not, suspicious, change indeed.

"Yes that sounds wonderful. I have a couple places in mind," she replied.

"Good," he paused. "Hopefully you can make it quick. I don't want to be out in that cold any longer than necessary."

He nodded and lifted his paper once more. As he pretended not to notice her stare, Samantha couldn't help but grin. For all his shrewd behavior and reckless tantrums, she knew the man underneath the façade pretty well. He was a standoffish dog. On the surface he seemed cold and angry, but underneath, was a decent man. It was her ever present hope, that she one day manage to bring that man out to the surface full time.

She smiled to herself and returned to her reading.

~

Breakfast had flown by. The mess of the kitchen had been cleaned and they both managed to get cleaned and dressed for the day. Their outfits were heavy, the cold of the day prompted for extra insulation. As they closed the door to their townhouse behind them, the chill of the air came rushing forward.

"Shit," Henry declared. Samantha grabbed his arm and pulled herself closer. He looked down to her with a satisfied grin, and together they began to wander the sidewalks. Along the streets, passed carriage after carriage, but each of them seemed already occupied. And so, they continued to walk.

    The downtown district was bustling with excitement. Gas powered lamps had been hung at various perches, providing a bit of light to an otherwise gloomy day. Just a few feet ahead sat the most popular toy store in the city. FAO Schwarz.

    "Let's try there," Henry suggested. He quickly guided them towards the entrance, ignoring the wealth of people coming and going, and barged inside. At last the cold had ended. Warm air populated the over populated store. He let out a sigh of relief and shook himself free of Samantha's grip. His eyes scanned the surroundings and immediately he could feel regret crawling over him.

    "Let's make this quick." He whispered. His eyes scanned the madness ahead with dread and despair. The notion of spending much time in a place so filled with people made his nerves twitch.

    She nodded in agreement and began to lead them down the various isles. There was so much to see, but with all the people, it was hard to actually get a close look at things. She tried her best to peer around people, sometimes even standing on her tip toes, but until people actually moved, her vision remained blocked.

Henry looked around, shrugging with aggravation, then decided to move to a different spot. Her willingness to put up with the hectic isle was her business, he had no interest in partaking in the mayhem. He moved down, past the stuffed animals and turned to the left. Building blocks. As a child his favorite toys had been the ones that required him to use his imagination. If anything seemed like a good purchase for her nephew, it would be something that pushed the mind a bit.

He stepped into the isle with the blocks and Lincoln logs. To his dismay, it was surprisingly empty. It seemed strange, but he opted not to let it sway his thinking. Slowly, he began to scan the various shelves, inspecting each set with careful precision. After a few minutes of careful observation, he realized that the store was actually quiet. The noise and mayhem seemed to have faded.

"Weird," he whispered to himself. He turned around and looked around the isle. There was no one in sight.

"Samantha?" He called out. His footsteps subtly filled the air as he began to move down the aisle. Turning a corner, he noticed that the next aisle over was also empty. The store was empty.

"What the fuck?"

He quickly dashed to the front of the store. Like the aisles, the register lanes were empty. The air was mute apart from the faint hum of the lights. They whispered to him a lullaby of contempt. In the distance he suddenly noticed the sound of paper being crumpled.

"Hello?" He wailed. His feet carried him towards the sound before his mind really had time to think about it. His curiosity was building, stacking itself so high that if he did nothing, it would fall. He had no choice but to surrender to the will of his courageous feet. The distant commotion continued to escalate. Over and over, the sound replayed. An ominous soundtrack in a place designed to feel festive.

"Who's there?" He questioned. Slowly he turned a corner and stepped back into the aisle with the blocks. Standing there, turned around, was a man. His face was hidden but his outfit was certainly on the unique side.

"Who are you?" Henry questioned. The man remained silent and still. Henry looked towards him with suspicion. Someone had been ripping paper, and yet, he could see no traces of paper anywhere near. The man stood still.

"Hey mister can you hear me?" He began to slowly move forward. With each step he could feel his anxiety continue to grow. There was something off about this man. About this whole situation. The closer he crept towards him, the heavier the air seemed to feel. There was a smell lingering around him. Like charcoal or something burned. *Screw this*, he thought to himself. He slowly began to back up, keeping his eyes locked forward until he had put a comfortable distance between the two of them. Finally, he turned around, only to notice a small pile of sand on the floor. Behind him, the sound of paper being ripped started once more. It seemed almost deafening.

"What the hell's the matter with you?" Henry yelled as he turned back towards the man. As he looked forward, he gasped, stumbling back and landing on the floor with a painful thump. The man was horrendous. A deformity unlike any he had ever seen. Cracked skin, empty eyes and sewn-shut mouth. The man began to saunter towards him.

"Shit!" Henry bellowed. He pushed himself back as quickly as he could. As he continued to retreat, he could feel the grains of sand rubbing against his palms. He paid it no mind. Urgently he continued to slide. Suddenly, the man stopped and lifted his hands. Henry peered with concern. The man continued to hold his hands up, as he did, a bit of dust began to form in his palms. It fell to the floor and quickly slithered towards him.

"It's you," Henry said with realization. At that moment, the sound of commotion returned.

"Are you alright sir?" A young man with a Santa hat asked. He reached down and held out his hand towards Henry.

"Umm," Henry stammered. He looked up towards the man, delirious and winded. He slowly reached up and accepted the assistance. The young man gave him a firm and quick pull.

"What happened?" He questioned.

Henry shrugged as he glanced around the aisle.

"Nothing," Henry whispered. "I just fell."

Chapter 4

Stress was at an all time high as Jacob sat quietly in his seat aboard the ferry. The weekend had flown by far too quick, and with Christmas quickly approaching, things were beginning to feel rambunctious. The whole of the weekend had been spent trying to figure out gifts for his siblings and nieces. Normally he enjoyed shopping for others. There was something so utterly satisfying about watching someone light up. But ever since that night at the diner, he found himself dreadfully distracted.

As a large wave crashed against the side of the ferry, Jacob found himself tipping. As he pushed himself back upwards, he noticed Henry in the distance. He stood next to a few others, joking back and forth about god knows what. Jacob peered as he noticed a small scratch on Henry's arm that looked like it had been done by a tree branch. *This is all his fault.*

He stood, and contemplated approaching, but as laughter emerged from Henry, he opted not to. Trying his best to keep his balance, he returned to his seat and sighed, the image of the man from the streets quickly coming and going from his mind. The whole experience had been like an infection. One that was quite rapid. It was all he could think about.

~

An icy wind cut through as everyone began to disembark from the ferry. The entrance to the immigration office wasn't far ahead, and yet, it still seemed a horrendous walk. The bitter bite of the arctic breeze stole all enjoyment from the once exciting surroundings. In fact, the sting of winter had that effect on almost all parts of life to Jacob. For so long he had dreamt of living in warmer climate. But each time he pondered a move, his mind raced to his mother. She was ill and beginning to take a turn towards elderly status. He sighed as the island's glacial breath soared towards him.

"Get a move on!" A voice abruptly called out. Jacob turned and grinned as he noticed one of his few friends approaching. Steve Hollinsworth. He was a jock type; tall, sturdily built with a short haircut. He and Jacob hadn't known each other long. Only a few months in fact, but there was a clear connection between the two. Both of them seemed naturally good hearted, a quality unfortunately missing from most of the men employed here.

"Seriously its freezing," Steve remarked. "Why are you standing around?"

Jacob watched as Henry and his buddies continued to laugh. He shook his head with aggravation and turned towards his friend.

"It's been a long day," Jacob replied.

"We just got here," Steve laughed. Jacob lowered his head and shot his friend an aggravated stare.

"I know."

The two peered at each other, then eventually smiled. Steve gave Jacob a pat on the back and they began to move towards the entrance. Each step through the icy vortex brought a sting to the skin. One could almost feel their skin beginning to crack and chap under the effects of the dry air. Jacob kept his head down, and pushed onto the entrance. As they stepped inside, the both of them expelled sighs of relief. It was warm inside, not as warm as home, but far warmer than being out in the elements.

The employee entrance was somewhat cramped. A tight hallway with not much in the way of design. There were various doors that led to multiple areas, including a changing room where all the employees would get ready. Jacob squeezed his way through the crowd of workers, trying his best to remain as far away from physical contact as he could.

"So what did you do over the weekend?" Steve asked.

"Not much. It was too cold to really want to do much of anything," Jacob replied. "I did hang out with Marci for a bit."

Steve looked to him with excitement and gave Jacob's shoulders a squeeze.

"You sly dog. Did you guys do it yet?" He questioned.

"No," Jacob asserted. "It's not like that."

Steve scrunched his nose as he contemplated the confusion that was Marci and Jacob. The constant will-they, wont-they, thing the two had going on was trying to witness. Steve had time and time again encouraged his friend to aim for bit more than friendship, but for some reason Jacob never seemed receptive to the notion. If only he could've jumped in his shoes.

As they entered the locker area, they filed inside. It was already quite crowded, conversation and laughter filled the air. Jacob wandered over to his assigned and began to shrug his coat. Not too far down, he could see Henry. He seemed cocky as ever as he straightened up his uniform. Jacob sighed as he watched.

"What are you staring at him like that for?" Steve blurted out. Jacob turned and quickly proceeded to smooth his uniform out.

"You were looking at him like you have a bone to pick or something."

Jacob closed his locker and turned around.

"I saw something weird this weekend," he whispered. "Something impossible."

Steve's eyes widened with curiosity.

"What?"

"You're not going to believe me, but I think I saw that man. Ya know, the one that died a couple months back," Jacob replied.

"Ummm," Steve paused. "Well you're not making much since. You said it yourself. The man died."

"I know," Jacob retorted. "That's what makes it what I saw all the more troubling."

He looked back towards Henry and noticed that he was fiercely scratching his arm, through his shirt. From the looks of it, it seemed to be the very same spot where he had seen the earlier scratch.

"Hmm," Steve smirked. "You're losing it buddy."

He grinned and offered a slight chuckle.

The monotony of the job was beginning to wear thin after only a couple hours. One person at a time, Jacob probed and questioned. But throughout it all, his mind kept focusing on the strange looking man he had seen in the streets. His thoughts were so focused on that, that for a moment, he thought he had seen him again. But this time, he looked normal, as he had that day in line. As it turns out, it wasn't him, but still, his presence lingered.

"Welcome to America," Jacob solemnly smiled. He handed over a stack of papers to a grateful woman with two children. She looked to him with a cheerful smile, then motioned for her children to move forwards.

Jacob paused and looked over at one of the other inspectors. Apparently he had a non English speaking customer because Henry stood there, looking arrogant as ever. As before, he seemed quite determined to scratch at his sleeve.

"Sir?" An middle aged man called out. Jacob turned forwards and suddenly, fell from his seat. He hadn't seen much, but he was fairly certain it was him again, the dead man.

"Jacob?" Steve questioned. He dashed over and offered him a hand. A couple booths over, Henry began to laugh.

"What happened?" Steve questioned.

"I saw him again," Jacob rebutted.

"Who?"

"The dead man," Jacob replied. From the distance, Henry's laugh began to fade and instead he found himself wearing a bit of concern. He peered towards Jacob with worry, then turned back towards the lounge where he had come from.

"There's no dead guy," Steve retorted. "You're just seeing things."

He gave Jacob a firm pull. As he returned to his feet, Jacob looked out to the crowd of immigrants. Steve was right, there was nothing unusual. He sighed with embarrassment, then looked to his friend.

"I guess you're right," he admitted.

"Hey, I usually am," Steve grinned. He turned around and began to head back to his booth, stepping in a small bit of sand as he did. Jacob tried his best to shake himself free of the ordeal, after all, he had a job to do. His focus turned reluctantly back to the crowd of desperate, and exhausted immigrants.

"Next."

Chapter 5

Henry awoke in the midst of the night feeling an irritating itch traveling through his arm. It had started a couple days ago, and no matter how much cream he put on, the sensation remained the same. Creeping from bed as silently as he could, he maneuvered his way to the bathroom and quietly pulled it open.

The candle inside flickered as he stepped within. He carefully reached towards it and held it up to his arm. The rash was continuing to grow, but still, he couldn't help but scratch at it. Slowly, he set the candle down and began to reach once again for the persistent problem spot. The relief was instant, but if he stopped for even a moment, the irritation returned. It was a vicious cycle that held him prisoner.

He sighed as he reached for a small bucket filled with water. Next to the bucket was a bar of soap. He reached for it, and began to wash at the spot. The suds brought an instant sting that surged through his arm and brought tears to his eyes.

"Shit," he gasped. Quick as he cold, he plunged his arm into the bucket and rinsed away the soap. The pain faded not too long after. It was like childhood all over again. Mom carelessly dumping peroxide atop even the smallest scraps. The sentiment was actually pleasant, a nice way to see himself through the moment. As he closed his eyes he could see her face, looking at him with love and concern as she nursed away his pain. She wasn't perfect, but even he couldn't deny the important role she played in his life.

As he opened his eyes he noticed the candle had reached the end of its wick. The subtle smell of smoke had begun to seep into the air, making it all the more obvious that darkness had arrived. He didn't bother to fidget or look around. That was the last candle and he knew it. He had really hoped to buy one of the newer lanterns that he kept hearing about, but with Christmas around the corner, money seemed a bit tight.

"Please."

His heart rate shot to a hundred in just a matter of seconds. Was the night simply playing a trick on him, or had he indeed heard something? He quickly reached around, searching for the handle.

"Please."

He paused once more. It seemed to be coming from the bathtub. From the corner, he could hear the faint sound of someone with weak breath.

"Who's there?" He whispered. He didn't turn around. His hand remained steadfast on the handle, ready to pull it open at a moments notice.

"Help," the voice moaned. The raspy breath drew nearer and the sound of footsteps quietly emerged. Henry desperately pulled on the handle, flinging the door open as he made a dash to the bed.

"Henry?" Samantha groaned. "What are you doing?"

He looked towards the open doorways, his heart still raced, he felt sick, as though he could throw up. The fear was paralyzing. Samantha grabbed his arm with concern and followed his desperate gaze. She studied the darkness of the doorway with curiosity. Even in the dark, she could sense Henry's fear. Something had shaken him quite terribly. He continued to study the opening, desperately listening for the heavy breaths, but there was nothing. A chill washed over him and he shuddered with concern.

"Nothing," he quipped. "Go back to sleep."

~

The following morning Henry awoke feeling exhausted and ill prepared for another day at the island. He had tried several times to fall asleep, but something always seemed determined to stop him. Be it the persistent rash, the unsettling experience in the bathroom, or the images of the man with the cracked skin.

"How did you sleep?" Samantha asked as she rolled towards him. She reached her arms across his stomach. It was warm, his slight amount of hair felt soft against her skin. She smiled as she felt his chest slowly rising up and down.

"Not great," he replied with an aggressive tone.

"Bad dreams again?" She questioned. Her hands continued to rub across his stomach and towards his arms. Suddenly, she felt something sticky. Quickly, she reeled back.

"What is that?" She abruptly questioned. She pulled her hand out from underneath the covers and noticed her hand was coated in a small amount of tacky blood that was quickly drying up.

"You're bleeding," she declared.

"I know," he calmly replied. He groaningly crawled out of the bed, revealing a blood-soaked blanket and sheet where he had laid. His arm was quite red with irritation and dried blood.

"Henry!" Samantha wailed. "What did you do to yourself?

He calmly glanced towards his arm and shrugged.

"There was something itchy under my skin. I think it was a piece of sand. I got though. I feel much better now," he answered.

"That's going to get infected."

She jumped from the bed and dashed towards him. Her eyes studied the damage for a moment. Without further conversation she reached for his hand and pulled him to the bathroom.

"We need to get that cleaned up."

As they stepped into the bathroom, she reached for the bucket of water and soap. She squinted for a moment as she noticed freshly wet foot prints decorating the floor. It had been hours since Henry came running to bed and yet, somehow the floor remained wet. It certainly piqued her curiosity but rather than feed him more of his paranoias, she opted to keep quiet. A nervous boyfriend is a distracted boyfriend. The holidays were no time to be distracted. She nonchalantly pushed a towel over top the evidence, then turned her focus to a neat stack of washcloths.

"What happened last night?" She questioned while carefully grabbing a cloth. She tossed it into the water and let it soak up a bit of moisture, then took a bar of soap and lathered it up. With the tenderness of a loving mother, she rubbed the towel against the dried blood.

"Ow," he hissed.

"Oh come on," she countered. "You need to be more of a man than that." She continued to wipe away the old blood, occasionally rinsing the cloth free of the blood.

Ten minutes passed, and what was once a mess of pain and irritation, now resembled a childhood cast. Her gauze wrapping skills leaved something to be desired, but she had covered the wound, that much was for sure. Henry looked to her with a grin. She was in the tub and slowly rubbing herself clean.

"The boys at work are going to like this," he laughed. He offered her a sincere smile. One of the first times in fact that she could ever recall seeing him display such an expression. It would've been off-putting, downright suspicious, had she not just babied him. He slowly leaned in for a kiss when a loud horn suddenly tore through the moment.

"Shit," Henry blurted as he quickly pulled away. Commotion started in the streets below, and all around them, raised voices could be heard through the walls. The work horn had been heard by all. The time for business was once again at hand.

"I have to get ready," he announced. He pulled the bathroom door open and stepped out towards the bed.

"I'm not so sure that's a good idea," Samantha called out. She splashed a bit of water onto her chest and began to lather up some of the soap.

"Someone's gotta pay the bills," he retorted.

She continued to splash about in the tub, it was cold and the water was quite limited, but it would still make do. She only needed to be presentable and smell fresh. The men at work were so easy to please, especially Mr. Jefferies. *Nothing more than a pervert*, she had said about him. Much to her disappointment, this didn't seem to bother Henry.

"Most men are," he had replied. It was in that moment when she truly realized that she was expected to amount to. Eye candy. She might also be trusted with taking notes, but not much else.

"You're not the only one with a job you know," she called out. In the other room, she could hear the sound of drawers being pulled open as Henry rummaged around looking for clothes.

"I don't need your help," he retorted.

"Not from what I've seen," she whispered. After the suds had all been rinsed off, she stepped out of the tub and onto the floor. Water slowly trickled down her legs and buttocks and soaked into the towel she had tossed down. She looked down at the dampness and pondered the wet footprints she had seen.

"Can you find a towel?" She questioned. Henry let out a rather obvious sigh of complaint, then began pulled open a closet. She stood cold and naked as she waited, trying her best to push aside his ridiculous demeanor.

"Here," he declared. She reached to the floor and picked up the towel he had begrudgingly tossed. It looked dirty and the crusty texture seemingly confirmed the notion. Nevertheless, she patted herself off. She quickly grabbed a towel and began to pat herself dry, then wandered out into the bedroom.

"You didn't have any clean ones?" She questioned. He turned, shrugged, and continued buttoning up his suit.

"You need to have a doctor look at that. I'm concerned you might get an infection. Lois at work had a husband lose his arm from nothing more than a cat scratch."

She tossed the towel to the floor and wandered over to a small suitcase she had left on the side of the bed. Inside, she had stored a hair brush, some perfume and a blue dress. She withdrew the dress from inside, then felt around for her corset. It was dreadfully uncomfortable, but it helped hold in her gut. If you didn't look like a toothpick, you weren't going to make it far in the secretary world.

"We have doctors on the island," he replied. He turned and watched as she worked to secure the corset around her waist.

"A hand please."

He groaned and approached. He began to snugly secure the ties while looking out the window towards the streets. There were kids playing a game with a ball right in the middle of the road. *Idiots*, he thought to himself. Once the ties were secured we wandered to the bed and sat.

"You know I did spend some time cleaning your arm and wrapping it. Maybe you could not act like such a jerk when I ask for a little help," she suggested. She lifted the blue dress up above her head and let it fall down atop her breasts.

"I mean it's only fair," she added. Her arms reached up and pulled the dress all the way down, then she turned to him and smiled.

"I can't help it. I just get so irritated."

"I know," she smirked. She slyly approached and planted a kiss onto his lips, then pressed her right foot against his crotch.

"But baby, if you don't stop the tough guy shit," she paused and applied a bit of pressure to his groin. He squirmed with discomfort and his cheeks turned red.

"You won't need a woman because you won't be a man."

He looked to her with the bashfulness of a boy caught peeping, then nodded.

"Let's get going," she declared.

They made their way out of the apartment and locked the door behind them. She pausd and waited for him, then grabbed his arm. Together they maneuvered their way past the homeless that had taken shelter inside. It was grosteque and uncomfortable to see, but with the themperatures being so low, one could hardly blame them. The stairs at the end of the hall were a good distance away, they would have a lot of bodies to step over before they reached a safe spot. Samantha pulled herself closer as they moved down the dreary halls, the floor dwellers made her nervous. Their desperation made them unpredictable and in some cases, violent.

Things were dark as they emerged at the foot of the stairs. The light from the sun wasn't allowed in the halls, the bums had seen to that. The grimness was their best chance at privacy and a dark night. The windows had been smashed and replaced with wood planks making the once elegant apartment seem not too unlike a tenement.

The sounds of the carriages in the streets creeped to to them, reminding them of their goals and their upcoming safety. They quickly moved down the halls and as they neared the door, Samantha pulled back, letting him open it. Like any good gentleman, he did. She stepped out onto the sidewalk and waited. It took only a few minutes for a carriage to come to a halt, her looks surely having nothing to do with it. As the horses came to a stop, Henry moved from the doorway and into the streets next to Samantha. There was a clear look of disappointment on the drivers face as the realization that she wasn't traveling alone set in.

"She needs to get to the Franklin building," Henry paused. "And I'm headed to the island."

"No problem," the driver replied through a fake smile. Henry handed the man some coinage, then pulled the door open for Samantha to step inside. She quickly scooted to the far side of the carriage, then Henry stepped inside.

"Ha," the driver called to the horses. He gave them a light crack of the reins and onwards they went.

The carriage ride was silent, they seemed more interested in the busyness of the streets than each other. Henry looked down towards the bandage as he realized the sudden desire to itch the wound had once again returned. In fact, it was a rather nagging sensation, but with her sitting so close, he didn't dare attempt to reach for it. He looked to her and smiled as a bit of sweat formed atop his forehead.

"What?" She smiled.

"We're at your stop," he replied. The carriage stopped and he eagerly jumped out. The Franklin building was large and grandiose, a mammoth creation and very popular place. It employed many housewives as well as young ambitious men that had a flair for numbers. It would've been a steady place for employment, but the politics and ass kissing were just far too much for Henry to deal with. As she stepped outside, he gave her a quick hug, then pulled back.

"Have a good day," he grunted. She attempted to hold him a moment longer, but he expertly weaseled his way out of the hug and back into the carriage. As he closed the door he noticed she was standing with her arms crossed and a displeased look upon her face.

"Leave the bandage alone," she called out as the carriage began to pull away. He nodded with understanding, then looked down at his arm. The roads were rough, puddles and dips littered the road, making for a mostly stressful commute, but still it beat walking.

"Fuck," he whispered. He reached for the gauze and began to unwrap it. Each turn he could feel his excitement rising. Satisfaction was quickly approaching.

"Whoa," the driver called out. The carriage came to an abrupt halt. Henry stopped and looked out the opening. They were back near his apartment once more. All around the streets wandered people with purposes. Be it work, fun or exercise, everyone seemed steadfast to their reasons for being out. A clap of thunder filled the air, and moments later it had begun to drizzle.

Henry quickly turned his attention back to the gauze and continued to unravel Samantha's hard work. He could practically hear her words in the air as he pulled it off and tossed the bloody rags onto the floor. The wound looked far more infected that it had earlier, but there was still something about it that brought an itch. It was unmistakable. His fingers reached towards the wound and began to scratch once again. Blood and flesh became lodged under his nails as he persistently began to dig. Soon his arm had a steady stream pouring down and dripping onto the carriage floor.

"Come on," he grunted as he continued to dig. Before long he was a centimeter into the flesh, but still the tingling remained. He continued to search the flesh for the cause, even after the carriage began to move again.

"Deeper," a grim voice instructed. Henry turned and suddenly began to tremble as he noticed the man with cracked skin sitting next to him. All across the surface of his skin were cracks and pieces of dry skin flaking off and dropping gently to the floor. His eyes, were focused on the wound.

"Shit," Henry jolted. He shot back and reached for the door to the carriage. The wheels had just begun moving but he didn't care. He jumped out the door and into the muddy streets.

"Oh my god," a startled woman cried out. She grabbed her child's hand and quickly pulled him away.

"Help me," Henry pleaded. He reached towards her, extending his bloodied arm out. She looked to him with contempt and fear, then began to wander towards a nearby building.

"Please," he whispered. The itchiness flared up and he urgently reached towards his arm. Only this time it was the opposite arm that presented the unpleasant sensation. He plunged his nails towards his skin and began to persistently dig for the cause. Harder and harder, deeper and deeper, he rummaged through the layers of his skin.

"Oh my god!" An elderly man bellowed. "Somebody help!"

Henry ignored the commotion, his mind was fixated on finding the cause of the tingling. Blood began to pour from his left arm. Soon, he was well into the flesh, but still the sensation remained. A persistent form of torcher with seemingly no end. His focus was relentless, nothing could shake him from the desire for relief, not even the police officer that slowly approached whilst yelling out cries for attention.

"Sir, what in the hell is the matter with you?" The large bellied officer asked. Henry continued to dig into his arm, then suddenly, moved to scratching his legs.

"You're hurting yourself son," the officer pleaded. "Sir!"

His words might as well been a thousand miles away. They were nothing but tiny footprints walking across a windy desert. All he could hear, all he could focus on, was the wound. The tiny specks of sand that danced within. He had to get them out. *They could cause an infection*, he thought. Layer after layer he dug. Behind him, stood the man with the cracked skin. He stood with his limbs contracted in a most unnatural way. All the while he whispered. Whispered to Henry.

"A little deeper," he instructed. "Keep going."

Finally, the officer had seen enough. He reached to his billy club and lifted it high. With a quick motion he brought it cautiously over Henry's head. He toppled over. His breathing was shallow, his wounds festering and secreting copious amount of scarlet red blood.

Chapter 6

There was an unmissable amount of grimness to the air today. All around the city, people spoke of the man who went crazy in the middle of the streets. Jacob had heard the rumors, but it wasn't until he returned to work that he found out the man in question was indeed his coworker Henry. He had never known Henry to be a skittish man, an asshole perhaps, but skittish not in the slightest. And yet, something vexed this audacious man, turned him into the town fool.

Cries of pain and agony filled the desolate halls of the Manhattan State Hospital. It was clearly a place of suffering, pain and agony. Most of the rooms were occupied with people that had been deemed mentally unfit for society. After Henry's display in the streets a couple weeks back, that's exactly what he was considered. Mentally unfit. He had been terminated, lost his apartment, and his girlfriend all in a matter of days. And yet, despite how crude of a person Jacob considered Henry, he had to push it aside. There was something about the timing of this mental breakdown that seemed utterly too strange.

"Sir," a young nurse called out. Jacob stood from his seat and nervously approached the curtesy desk.

"Dr. Gordon will see you now," she informed. She smiled and sauntered from behind the counter. He returned her sincerity with as much of a grin as he could muster.

"Your friend was in real bad shape," she explained as she lead him down the hall. "He's lucky to be alive."

"He's not my friend," Jacob whispered.

"Oh," she paused. "Then how do you know him?"

Jacob shuttered as every painstaking day working next to Henry rushed back to him.

"From work."

"Oh, I see. Well I have some coworkers here that I absolutely adore," she explained. "Maybe they aren't really friends though. I don't know. It's all so confusing. I mean is it weird to call your coworkers friends?"

Jacob ignored the question and kept his eyes trained forwards.

"I mean if it were me, and I were in your shoes, I would definitely call anyone I care about enough to come to this place, a friend."

"How much further?" Jacob questioned.

"It's just up a couple more doors. Anyways some of the people here, are kind of weird ya know?

Maybe you have to be kind of strange to work in a loony bin. I mean not that this is a loony bin anymore. No sir, we call ourselves a hospital. Don't want the patients feeling labeled."

She stopped outside a door and pushed it open to reveal a bed and a man secured to the bed with straps. Standing just inside the door was a tall gentlemen with a white coat and a handlebar mustache.

"Dr. Gordon can help you with the rest of your concerns," she smiled and waved him through. Jacob squirmed past her and stepped inside the room, extending his hand towards the stern looking doctor.

"Thank you Shannon," Dr. Gordon nodded. She giddily smiled and exited the doorway.

"So Mr. Daffren what can I do for you?" he asked.

Jacob gulped and looked towards Henry who seemed to be in a deep sleep judging by the movements of his corneas.

"Well I know this man, we work together and well, they are talking about firing him. My boss wanted me to check on him to see if he's going to be fit to work soon." He grinned to himself as he considered how convincing the lie must've seemed. He hadn't planned on lying, but something about the situation made a tall tale sound exciting.

"Heavens no sir," Dr. Gordon chuckled. "This man is under the delusion that some dead man with has been stalking him and telling him that he needs to dig into his flesh to relieve an itch. He calls him the *Itch Man*."

He turned and looked towards Henry with a heavy, solemn expression.

"Your friend is not well."

He's not my friend, he thought once again. He opted not to express his thoughts and instead strolled over towards the bed side.

"Can he talk?" Jacob asked.

"Well he's a bit sleepy, but it's been a few hours since his last sedative. I'm sure he'll come around soon enough," Dr. Gordon replied.

"Why don't you stay and visit for a bit, he doesn't get many. I have other rounds to make but I can come check on you guys in ten or fifteen minutes."

"That would be great," Jacob retorted.

"Excellent. I will leave you to it." With that, the doctor promptly made his way out the room, leaving Jacob alone with the unconscious shell of a once intimidating bully. He looked down towards the bandages covering his arms and legs and hesitated. A part of him wanted to see the damage, to see exactly what a mental breakdown really looked like, but another part of him still feared him. Even in his unconscious and restrained state, he still managed to see a juggernaut.

Screw it. He slowly reached towards the left arm and began to gently tug at the bandage. It was held on but worn out tape so it came loose rather easily. He gulped and studied Henry's senseless face. Taking a deep breath, he began to unravel the wrap. He kept his actions slow and methodical. The last thing he needed was to wake up a mad man. Over and under, he unwrapped the bandage, when an abrupt sound like a gust of wind passed behind him.

"Shit," he joltingly said as he turned around. Hanging on the wall was a chalk board with some notes from the various doctors, some drawings of the outside, and a small photograph of a young woman he assumed to be Samantha. He hadn't met her, but like all the workers on the island, he'd heard plenty about her.

"I've got that bitch wrapped around my finger," Henry had flaunted. *How the mighty fall.*

He shrugged and turned around. Henry was looking straight at him. His eyes wide as the day long.

"You're awake," Jacob noted. Henry remained silent, looking at him like a child that had been denied a treat. There was hint of fear in his expression, he studied Jacob with steadfast persistence.

"The doctor tells me you're seeing things. Seeing a man who you say is dead." He took a few steps closer, but rather than follow his steps, Henry continued to stare off towards the wall. Jacob looked down towards Henry's fingers, which were twitching as though trying to reach for something.

"The Itch Man."

Henry's expression widened and his mouth opened wide. With his arms still restrained, he pointed his index finger towards the wall. Jacob looked down and gulped. There were breaths coming from behind him. It was warm and based on the force, it seemed as though someone were standing mere inches away. His hands began to shake and his skin began to flush. Slowly, with the temperament of a child peeking under the bed, he turned around. As before, there was nothing but a chalk board with random notes.

"You had me scared for a minute," Jacob sighed. He let out a forced chuckle, but then, he noticed something strange. The photo on the wall, the one that he had saw just barely a minute ago, was gone. In its place, there was a small crude drawing of the Itch Man. At the bottom it read, *the only way to be free is to itch*. He shuddered and turned back towards

Henry. Both arms had been unwrapped and the wounds were once again oozing blood. Henry had somehow gotten loose. In his hands, he held a piece of paper that he rubbed back and forth across his wrist.

"What the fuck?" Jacob sneered. Wasting no further time, he turned and dashed towards the door. In the background, he could hear the persistent sound of Henry rubbing the paper back and forth across his skin.

"Jacob wait!" Henry called out. He stopped in the doorway. His heart was racing like a locomotive and his forehead had begun to sweat. His hands trembled, and everything in him down to his very core told him to keep moving, but he couldn't, he felt stuck, held hostage by the grotesque situation. He haltingly turned around. Blood was pooling all over the floor as Henry stood with wide arms and a mortified look on his face.

"He's coming for you," he whispered. "You'll itch soon. We all will."

Suddenly, he plunged a fountain pen into his chest. He pushed it back and forth, up and down his flesh as hard as he could. Blood spurted all over the floor and before long, he fell to the floor.

Chapter 7

Jacob burst through the hospital doors and dropped to his knees as he took a deep breath. It was frigid, snow had begun to fall in heavy, wet clumps, but he didn't care. What he had just witnessed transcended anything he'd ever expected to see in his life. Sure, everyone had heard of the crazies in the loony bin, but this was something different. Supernatural even. How had Henry been restrained in a bed one moment, and then free the next?

"He could've killed me," he whispered to himself. Around him, people both came and arrived. Those who were arriving had smiles, those that were leaving did not, but none of them experienced quite the flow of emotions he had. None of them had witnessed unspeakable evil. The Itch Man had been there, he was sure of it. Nothing else made sense. And hell, even the idea of a dead Japanese man walking around whispering dark orders into someone's ears didn't make sense. By all rights it seemed nonsensical.

"You there," a stern voice called from behind him. Jacob turned and noticed a cranky security guard approaching.

"What the hell happened in there? The doctor wants to ask you some questions."

Jacob climbed to his feet and wiped the snot from his nose, looking the guard over for any sign of a weapon. He tossed his hands into the air and began to back away.

"I'm not going back in there. No way in hell," Jacob replied. At that moment from the main entrance emerged another guard, this one looked far larger and even more temperamental.

"The doctor just wants to ask you some questions. We've got a patient bleeding out and you were the last one to see him," the second guard explained.

"Look," Jacob paused. "I didn't do anything. I'm telling you it was like nothing I've ever seen before. One minute he was restrained and the next he wasn't."

Shut up you fool or they'll toss you in here too!

"There's something weird going on in there and I'm not sticking around to find out."

The two guards took a few steps closer and withdrew their revolvers.

"I'm not asking again," the second guard declared. Jacob looked to them with concern, but suddenly something caught his eyes. On the ground, amongst the wet piles of snow was a small trail of sand that weaved in and out of the various puddles.

"He's here," Jacob whispered. With that, he turned around and made a mad dash for the streets. Behind him, he could hear the cries and screams of the two guards. Guns were being fired, but none of the shots came anywhere near him.

Once he arrived at the main district of shops, taverns and restaurants he stopped to catch his breath. His heart was racing so fast it seemed capable of exploding at any moment. The exhaustion was so severe he felt certain he was going to pass out. There was a sharp pain in his side and his fingers and toes were frozen but none of that paled in comparison to the fear filling his mind. Anxiety had given him a stamina he hadn't previously been capable.

"Jesus Christ," he exhaled. "That fuckers real."

He looked to the streets ahead and gulped. *I've gotta see Marci.* His legs found their strength once more. The walkways were crowded with people doing last minute shopping. Christmas was only a couple days away. Soon the city would be filled with joyful bells and praise. He cut into the road, narrowly missing a carriage and began to charge forward. The horse pulling the carriage behind him let out a startled neigh, and lifted its front legs.

"Hey you fucking asshole you scared my horse!" A man yelled. Jacob ignored him and continued forward. He made a quick turn down Madison avenue and then crossed back onto the sidewalk. There was still a plethora of people but it seemed a bit more spaced out this time. The diner where Marci worked at wasn't far ahead, he knew it all too well. He quietly made his way down the sidewalks, hoping all the while his friend was actually working.

As he reached the entrance to Billy's he paused and looked through the window. Just as he had hoped, Marci was working. She was walking towards a family with her arms full of plates and a stressed look upon her face. For a moment he almost considered turning around and leaving, she seemed to be going through a rough night, but he needed her. Needed their friendship. He pushed the door open and stepped inside.

The atmosphere was loud with commotion. Apparently as it grew closer to Christmas it made people want to cook less. He scanned the restaurant for an open table, but there didn't seem to be any. *Shit*. He shrugged away his frustration and marched towards her.

"Jacob," she said with surprise. "What's wrong? You look pale."

He leaned closer and grabbed her arm.

"I need to talk to you. Its urgent," he said with a solemn stare. She looked to him for a moment and then looked over to another woman who was taking orders from customers.

"Barb can you cover my tables for a couple minutes?" She questioned. The elderly woman nodded with aggravation, then turned around.

"We need to be quick. Barb can't handle a rush," Marci explained. She led Jacob into the back kitchen and then towards a large door that housed the pantry. As they stepped inside she approached one of the gas lanterns and ignited it. The light was minimal but it was certainly better than the darkness.

"I went to the institution today to see Henry," Jacob whispered.

"How was he?" She inquired.

"He's real Marci. The Itch Man is real," he grabbed her hands and held them firm.

"I've seen him twice now, and Henry did too. That's what made him go crazy."

Marci released his hands and took a couple steps back.

"You don't believe me?"

"Jacob. What are you talking about is a very difficult thing to believe. And further more what is the connection between this man you think you saw and Henry?" She questioned.

"Henry went crazy from his guilt. That's all."

Jacob shook his head with agitation and took a step closer.

"I think somehow Itoro Itcheman survived. Or maybe he didn't. Maybe he was brought back. But whatever the reason, he's coming after the people who were there that day."

He sighed as his hands began to shake.

"Henry told me the Itch Man was coming for me and that soon I'd itch too."

Marci laughed and put her hand to her mouth, shaking her head with disbelief.

"You can't actually believe that."

"You didn't see what I saw today. Henry was unconscious one minute, and the next he had escaped from his restraints and began stabbing himself to get to relieve an itch."

"That sounds awful," Marci agreed. "But it's all just a symptom of his delusion. You're making yourself paranoid. Perhaps you're feeling guilt the same way Henry did."

"Why would I feel guilty?" He barked. "I did everything I could to make sure that man made it into the country. I didn't have anything to do with what happened."

The sound of a plate crashing against the ground suddenly tore through the air, followed by laughter and some back and forth arguments.

"I have to get back out there," Marci sighed. "I swear I don't know why that old lady works here."

She pushed open the door to the pantry and stepped into the kitchen. Monty, the young cook who had immigrated with his family a few years back was sweating as he rushed back and forth to get food prepared. She peered her head out towards the dining area and held her finger up to Barb.

"You'll be okay right?" She asked. She turned to Jacob and shrugged with guilt.

"Yea. Yea I'll be fine. You just get back to work. We can catch up later," he replied. She took a step towards him and offered him a firm, but brief hug, then turned around and dashed back out into the dining area.

"Hey mister," Monty called out. "If you're going to be back here how about you put on an apron and help."

Jacob peered at him with confusion, then retreated from the kitchen. The dining room was even more packed than it was just a bit ago. On the floor was some broken glass which had yet to be swept up and standing in the doorway were two more people waiting patiently for a table. He carefully maneuvered past them and stepped out into the street.

The streets were covered with a thick layer of snow and more continued to trickle down, despite that, signs of travel were still quite evident. Footprints and tire tracks littered the ground, leaving small bits of dirt and brick visible. A leopard spotted road, masked in an artic chill. Jacob pulled his jacket tight as a breeze soared towards him. It tried with desperation to deter him, to freeze him out. He was quite lucky however, that his apartment wasn't far off, just thirty minutes, but with the snowy weather, even thirty minutes seemed long.

Keep moving, he thought to himself as he plowed through the unkind conditions. His heart raced with each dark alley and empty lot, he couldn't help but expect to see his tormentor standing like a snowman in the midst of it all. Henry's threat had affected him in a very real way. He felt uneasy, nervous and even occasionally thought he was feeling itchy.

Twenty-five minutes passed and as expected, he finally arrived at the rough looking building he called home. Not that long ago the whole place was considered a place for the poor, now it seemed a little more refined, although still not very special. He quickly climbed the steps and pulled against the door. It hesitated for a moment, held tight by ice, but eventually, with a firmer tug, creaked open. Warmth. At least warmth. He looked the halls over and swiftly dashed towards the stairs.

By the time he reached his apartment door, his hands had begun to sting, the sensation of being cold, then warm, was never a pleasant one. He reached into his pocket, pulling out his key and then inserting it into the lock. With a twist and a push, the door opened.

A strong rush of wind blew past as he stepped inside. A window had apparently been left open. Shit. He kicked off his shoes, then hastily ran towards the unexpected opening. The floor was wet, snow had melted and now his socks were wet as well. He pulled the window down as firmly as he could, then looked towards the squishy carpet.

"Damnit," he muttered. He hadn't gotten around to doing laundry yet, so at the moment all his clothes were decidedly dirty. Still, dirty socks were better than wet ones. He strolled over to a hamper and picked around until he found a dry pair. They stunk, he pulled them back with disgust, then quietly pulled them onto his feet. After his feet had been properly dressed, he reached for a towel and pulled one out.

Dirty, just like the socks but he only needed to soak up a bit of water. Nothing a dirty towel couldn't handle. He tossed the towel atop the carpet and watched as the red of the towel turned a bit darker.

"I don't remember leaving that open," he muttered. Paranoia, his newfound friend, fed him all kinds of thoughts. Someone had been there, someone had broken into his apartment through his window. How else could it have been open? It wasn't him. He was quite sure. He winced at the notion of a break-in, then glanced around the apartment. It was quite dim, but thankfully his lantern still had some gas. Sitting on the table was a book of matches, he carefully tore one out and gave it a strike. The lantern ignited and the walls lit up with shadows.

Silence. Gloominess. Lonely. He sat on his bed, looking towards the night sky and wondering about all he had done so far. The mistakes, the regrets. Isolation. So many of his friends had found partners, and yet, he didn't have one. Was Marci, the one for him? The thought had frequently entered his mind. He stood up, looking towards his dresser, at the photo the two of them had taken last summer. What a great summer that had been. She had taken the day off work, canceled her family plans and hung out with just him. It was the closet thing to a date that they had ever had.

He smiled as he thought back to a moment they had shared on the shoreline. Sitting and watching dog walkers, making up stories for each of them. There were so many types of people to see, so many stories to be told. He grinned, and closed his eyes. Suddenly, there was a loud thump at the door. Marci, he thought to himself.

"Well that was a short shift," he exclaimed as he pulled the door open. The hall was empty, no one was there and from the looks of the dried carpet, no one had been. He peered with confusion as he considered the plethora of possibilities behind the strangeness. The apartment building was home to some delinquent kids, kids that rather enjoyed playing pranks on people. It wasn't very common, but with it being dreadful outside, perhaps the season for pranks had returned.

"Hello?" He called out. There was nothing to be heard. No giggles, no whispers, no sounds from tiny feet. He shrugged and stepped back inside, closing the door with a bit of apprehension. As he made his way back to his bed, he could've sworn that he heard something. Subtle, but it did seem like the voice of a child. He turned around and quickly dashed back to the door, pulling it open in an accusatory fashion.

"I heard you," he exclaimed. Once again, the hall was empty. But this time, there were two footprints that stood just in front of the door.

"It's too late for games," he declared. He took a step out and inspected the carpet. There were no other footprints to be seen. They both stopped and started at his door. Just two. That was all. A bit of unease began to find him, and suddenly he could feel his heart beginning to race.

HARK THE HEARLD ANGLES SING!
GLORY TO THE NEW BORN KING!

The lyrics came so sudden that he tripped, falling to the ground and hitting his nose against the carpet. Blood quickly seeped like a faucet with a bad seal.

"Ugh," he grunted.

PEACE ON EARTH AND MERCY MILD!
GOD AND SINNERS RECONCILED!

His hands shook and his heart raced as he flipped himself over. Standing in the middle of his doorway was the Itch Man. He looked as he had before, gloomy and mysterious. He stared towards Jacob, then out his hand.

"Please," Jacob pleaded. "What do you want from me?"

The Itch man remained silent, from his palm, a bit of sand trickled down, landing on the floor in a small pile.

"Jacob?" A voice abruptly called. *Marci?* He jumped to his feet and dashed down the halls towards her.

"Run!" He called out.

JOYFUL ALL YE NATIONS RISE!

As he reached her side he gripped her shoulders and gave her a brief hug.

"You weren't lying," she whispered.

"We've got to go," he proclaimed. He turned her towards the stairs, in the window overlooking the streets, were the faces of three women, all with dark faces, all with red eyes. They sung the lyrics to *Hark The Harold* with a positive, yet unsettling tone. They would never be able to hear that song the same way again.

Down the stairs they dashed, all the while, the song continued, so loud that it was almost deafening. By the time they reached the bottom of the stairs, both of them were white with fear. Jacob continued to pull her arm, leading her towards the end of the hall.

"Wait," Jacob warned. A small tremor shook the floor, tossing bit of dirt into the air. Before long the air was filled with a fine dust, and from within the dust, a figure manifested. The Itch Man. He moved towards them and summoned the dust to follow in a trail behind him.

"That way's not gonna work," Jacob advised. They turned around, looking towards the stairs, then at a window which led to the street.

"Not the window," Marci pleaded.
*ITCH MAN COMES TO FREE YOUR BURDEN
ALL WILL ITCH WHEN HE RETURNS
PAINFUL PAINFUL CONSTANT ITCHING
YOU'LL FIND PAIN, YOU NEVER KNEW*

"We don't have a choice," Jacob retorted. He pulled her arm and jogged to the window. Behind them, the footsteps of the Itch Man grew louder. As they reached the window, Jacob lifted his leg, shattering the glass. He stuck his head outside and looked around.

"He's getting closer," Marci warned. She watched down the hall with anxiety, in front of the Itch Man, a small wave of sand traversed nearer and nearer.

Jacob pulled himself back, then looked to Marci.

"Climb," he ordered. Just on the other side of the window was a ladder that was to be used in emergency situations, particularly fires. It was wet, covered with ice and snow but it was their only way out, and the ground wasn't far off.

"Now!" He reiterated. He moved down the hall and pulled out a matchbook. His eyes met with the Itch Man's as he struck a match and threw it down. The carpet erupted in flames, and the sand, began to screech as though it were a dying hyena. Jacob swerved around and noticed that Marci had gotten clear of the window. He ran as fast as he could, paying no mind to the somber twist on Hark The Harold that filled the air. As he reached the window he looked down and noticed that Marci was safe and looking up towards him. He turned around and placed his foot onto the first step of the ladder. There was a thick smoke that filled the hallway and the fire had apparently been put out.

With his foot near the last step of the ladder, he jumped, landing firmly but onto his feet. The snow continued to fall heavy and the streets seemed rather abandoned. Then again, it was nearly ten at night and two days before Christmas, most people were likely with their families sitting listening to the evening tunes.

"So that's him?" Marci questioned. She looked terribly winded and disturbed.

Jacob looked to her with a shaken expression, and a tear dripped from his eye.

Chapter 8

"You shouldn't have been here," Jacob sighed. "I shouldn't have put you in danger. Its me he wants, I'm the one that was there when he died."

Marci casually approached and put her cold hands to his cheeks. They were quite chilly but it hardly affected him. His heart still raced and all he could feel was contempt for Henry and all he had caused. None of this would have happened if it were not for that ignorant man's racist actions.

"This is all Henry's fault. He's the one who tried to undo what I had done," he looked to the ground and exhaled as he recalled the sand that had been hidden in the man's luggage.

"But I'm the one that let him through in the first place. If I would've stopped him, all this wouldn't have happened."

"You didn't know what was going on. You were just doing your job, and being you. A good and honest man," Marci explained.

Jacob looked to the sky, letting the flakes fall down his face, it felt good, a necessary cool. He began to dwell on the past, on his sins and whether or not he could fully accept her kind words of praise. No one was perfect, he knew that better than most. His mother had been instrumental in teaching him that, her cruelty towards him trickled down from generation to generation, until it finally arrived to him.

"I'm not as honest as you think Marce," he replied. He continued to look to the sky, as his mind traveled his various hidden chambers.

"I lied to you."

He looked down to Marci and shrugged.

"There's more to the story."

Marci's expression suddenly shifted to concern.

"What do you mean?"

A carriage abruptly approached, coming to a stop and ending the moment.

"You folks need a ride?" The driver quickly asked.

Jacob pondered the present events, and suddenly realized the one person who could shed light on this, was the one who started it all. Henry. He had seen the Itch Man, even been told a message with which to pass on. Perhaps he knew something else. What else had he been told?

"Yes please," Jacob replied. "We need to get to the mental hospital."

Marci squinted her forehead with confusion as she looked towards Jacob. What was he up to?

"Ah," the driver replied. "Well hop on in. I'll get you there just as quickly as I can."

Jacob gave Marci a nod, she paused for a second, then stepped into the carriage. Once they were both on board, the driver gave the horses a quick tug on the reins, and away they went. Jacob looked towards the apartment building, watching it fade from sight with a sigh of relief. Tonight had been strange, terrible actually. It was time. Time to finally get some answers. The Itch Man seemed content on infecting him, but why?

The ride was silent, Jacob spent most of the time in his own little daze, dwelling on his earlier experience at the hospital. Prior to today, he had never before set foot in that place, and now, he was to be there twice in one day. What cruel irony was that? He studied the roadways, keeping track of their progress and how close they neared. Once it became clear that the destination was close, he looked to Marci and exhaled.

"We're almost there," he whispered. Marci's hands had begun to tremble, she looked to him with unease.

"What were you trying to tell me before we the carriage showed up? You said you lied. What did you lie about?"

Jacob nodded as the day at the island played in his mind. He had heard some commotion which pulled him away from his booth, soon, he realized what Henry had done.

"Itoro never made it past my booth. I turned him away," he admitted.

"What?" Marci pondered. "But you said that you had cleared him, and on his way to exchange his money is when Henry intervened."

Jacob shook his head in disagreement. Indeed, that was the story he had told her, hell perhaps even the story he had told himself, but it simply wasn't true. He had failed himself, failed his beliefs and betrayed his morality in favor of fear and paranoia.

"No. I never let him through."

His mind began to replay the day. Itoro had been in line and he had called him over with immediate reservations about his entrance into the country.

~

"What brings you to America?" He questioned. The Japanese man looked to him confused and shrugged. He wore a mask over his face and his hair was quite messy. His appearance was rather unkempt and his clothes looked more like a dress than anything a man should've been wearing. He studied the strange man, as he did, he looked to the others in line. Each of them looked more traditional, poverty stricken, but traditional.

"Why are you wearing that mask?" Jacob asked. One again the Japanese man shrugged, handing his papers over with no words of explanation. Atop the pile of papers was a note, hand written, from the looks of it by someone who understood English.

My mother is dying and I have come to help her transition to the next life. It is customary in my family to be buried with the sacred sands from the gardens of my ancestors.

As Jacob read the parchment, the man reached into his suit case, pulling out a jar of sand and pointing to it. Jacob raised his eyebrows with concern as he continued to observe the strange fellow. Everything about him seemed unready for America.

"We don't allow that kind of stuff to be brought into the country," Jacob explained. The Japanese man seemed once again, unphased by his words. There wasn't time for this, the line was long and there were many others in need of help. He needed to wrap this up, and quickly.

"I need a translator," he called into the air. A man standing guard towards the front of the line, nodded in understanding and then blew a whistle into the air. It was loud, bordering on deafening, but it did serve its purpose rather well.

The door to the far left, which held some offices, pulled open revealing Henry in all his stupid splendor. Jacob sighed. He would've preferred anyone to him. Henry hadn't been here long, but already he had proven himself to be a spiteful man.

"What language does he speak?" Henry questioned, coming to a stop and looking over the unkept immigrant.

"Take a guess," Jacob replied. He nodded towards the man and pointed towards the mask.

"I don't know why we was sent through wearing that. Also, he's carrying a strange jar of sand."

Henry looked the man over, then reached for the jar.

"Anata wa koko ni mochikomu koto wa dekimasen," he explained. *You can't bring that here.*

He held it up and shook his head disapprovingly.

"Watashi wa kore o toranakereba naranaidarou." *I'm going to have to take this.*

"Anata wa dekimasen," the man argued. *No, you can't.*

He quickly reached for the jar and retrieved it.

"Anata wa watashi no mono kara te o hanasanai." *You keep your hands off my stuff.*

Jacob waved over to a nearby security guard and pointed nervously to the *now* distraught man. Things had started to heat up between Henry and the man. The situation went from being a mild debate to a full-on struggle. The two men fought against each other, both of them trying to maintain control of the jar. As the guard approached, Itoro gave Henry a shove, pushing him to the floor and turning around with the jar and his bag.

"Stop sir," the guard called out. He began to jog towards him, then sternly grabbed his arm. Jacob watched the ordeal, feeling a bit of unease as all eyes locked onto them.

"Can we take this out of here?" Jacob questioned. He approached the guard with Henry in tow.

"Watashi wa koko ni iru no ga tadashī," Itoro exclaimed. *I have right to be here.*

Jacob shook his head, and handed over a packet of papers with a stamp that read *entrance denied*.

"Jissai ni wa anata wa shimasen," Henry sneered. *Actually you don't.*

Itoro gripped the papers with shaking hands, then twisted the top from his jar.

"Let go of the jar!" The guard yelled. He lifted his gun, aiming it towards Itoro with an air of nervousness creeping into his grip. Tension lingered in the air like a dump on a hot day, its effect sticking to each that were privy to see the altercation. All around the room, people began to panic, some of them even grabbing their bags and making their way to the exits. No one knew what the man was up to, but most didn't care to find out.

Itoro looked the three of them over, then lifted the jar towards them. He was going to throw it, that much was clear.

Bam! A gun went off. The thunderous commotion echoed against the walls, bringing a quick silence to all. Jacob looked to Henry and gulped. Itoro had been shot. Straight through the chest. The jar crashed to the ground and the sand seeped to the floor. Itoro fell to his knees as blood continued to drain from the wound. Tension filled the air. No one had anything to say. Everyone seemed stuck, mesmerized by the horrific scene.

"Dōshite?" Itoro groaned. He looked towards Henry with humiliation, sadness and perhaps most importantly resentment.

"Anata ga shiharau," he whispered. He slumped over, landing in a pile of his own blood. As the blood touched the sand, it began to animate, moving towards him and quickly encompassing his body.

"What the hell?" Henry questioned. The man quickly dissolved, the sand acting as some kind of decomposing agent. It didn't take long for there to be nothing but his robes remaining. He had vanished, like water in a cup left under the hot sun, he was no more.

Jacob stared at the ground with disbelief. It was like nothing he had ever seen. What substance could do that? Certainly there was more to that sand then they had realized.

"What was that stuff?" Jacob muttered. He looked to Henry, who stood speechless. He turned to him and shrugged as his eyes began to redden with guilt.

~

"Oh my god," Marci sighed. She looked towards the hospital and shuddered.

"You didn't do anything wrong though. Your job is based on suspicions. Your gut instinct is your only tool."

Jacob waved her words of comfort away. Suspicion was his job, true, but that day, he hadn't used suspicion. There was something more. Something less honorable motivating his actions. Fear. Fear that the man was up to something. Fear that his mask was an indication of him being contaminated. Fear that to let him in would spell diaster. And why? All because he was wearing a mask?

"I was being stupid. I read too much into a situation and caused a scene that never should've happened," Jacob retorted.

"I killed him."

Marci shook her head with disbelief.

"It's true. The moment I as I allowed paranoia to enter my thoughts, I had killed him."

The carriage came to a stop. Marci looked out the window and gulped. The stories of this place were infamous. A place of doom, insanity, and despair. The name had been changed, but that had don't very little for its reputation. *The crazy house*. It would always be that.

"We're here," the driver called out. Jacob nodded and pushed open the door. He stepped outside, landing quiet inconveniently in a deep pile of snow which quickly soaked his feet.

"Careful," he warned, offering Marci a gentle hand. She accepted the assistance and stepped down, landing in his previously left track.

"That'll be ten cents," the driver stated. He extended his hand like a child awaiting a treat. Jacob quickly reached into his pocket and pulled out the correct change, then handed it to the eager man.

"Be safe," the driver advised. "This place is not for the faint of heart. Most that go in, never come out."

Marci's hands trembled as she reached for Jacob.

"Are you ready for this?" he questioned. He looked to Marci and gave her a solemn nod.

"Is anyone ever ready to step into this place?" She countered.

"Stay close to me," he suggested. He tossed his shoulders back and moved towards the door. There was a weight to them he hadn't remembered feeling before, like a heard of elephants was pulling on them from the other side. He grunted with exhaustion, and gave them as firm a pull as he could muster.

"Whoa," Marci called out as Jacob went tumbling behind her into a pile of snow. The door remained wide open, taunting his efforts with its now weightless appearance.

"What the heck was that?"

Jacob looked up to her feeling a tad bit embarrassed. It had only been a few seconds, but already his bottom was feeling wet from the snow soaking into his pants. She looked down to him with a smile. He pushed himself up and wiped off the snow.

"That door felt like someone was pulling on it from the other side," he explained. It sounded like a convenient excuse designed to spare him humiliation, but then again, after all she'd seen today, who was she to question truths.

They stepped inside, but instead of being greeted by cheerful smiles, and words of welcome, they were meant only with dark. Darkness all around. The halls were dark, not a single lit lantern in the whole place. The desk, which normally housed someone to greet newcomers was vacant, although perhaps it was too late an hour for someone to be positioned there.

What little light that did exist, came from underneath doorways. The halls were lined with faint slivers of light. Each sliver hiding something. A patient, a closet, staff quarters.

"Is it normally like this?" Marci whispered. Jacob peered at her with obvious nervousness.

"I don't know. It sure doesn't seem right."

He grabbed her hand and slowly guided them down the hall to the left, the very one he had been in only a few hours ago. There were whispers coming from the various rooms. Sounds of madness and despair creeped around them, slowly making its way into their ears. As they pressed onwards, Marci tightened her grip, nothing had ever left her feeling this empty as much as this hall had.

The whole place felt like a vacuum, a place where positivity went to die. A bottomless pit for people who were ill equipped to function in society. The whispers continued. Shadows darted back and forth in the slivers of light. Their footsteps echoed against the walls, offering something to hear besides the whispers, but in truth it wasn't much better.

"I knew you would be back," a voice quietly proclaimed. A door on the left side of the hall slowly pulled open, revealing Dr. Gordon. There was a dim light seeping from the room that just barely illuminated his face, his eyes seemed suspicious and his grin quite coy.

"I have a good eye for the bad ones."

Jacob pushed aside the comment and took a few steps forward. Suddenly, he paused. His eyes looked the doctor over. There was a faint trail of blood that had followed him from the other room, it appeared to be coming from his right arm and left leg.

"What happened?" Marci questioned. Her skin began to tingle as an uneasy feeling began to creep into her.

"I think the answer to that question is best left for private," Dr. Gordon replied. He offered a not-so-subtle head tilt towards the door he had just entered from.

"I don't think so," Jacob argued. "Marci don't go anywhere with him. He's up to something."

Marci studied the doctor's expression and couldn't help but take note of an unusual eagerness to him. She had never met the man before, and certainly the hospital was an ominous setting for a first-time rendezvous, but oddly enough, she felt compelled.

"I'll be fine Jacob," she whispered. Jacob turned to her aghast. Surely, she had to see the fact that he was bleeding.

"Marci," he began. "Look at him, he's covered in blood."

"I'm sorry but I have to insist," Dr. Gordon retorted. Marci studied him once more, then took a step towards the doorway.

"Marci," Jacob called out. At that moment, Dr. Gordon lunged forwards, tackling Jacob to the ground.

"Run dear run!" The doctor called out. She stood still with confusion when all of a sudden, the light from within the room vanished, leaving darkness in the halls once more. Everything was dark, there was nothing but the grunts of the two men wrestling on the floor.

"Get out of here!" The doctor called out once more. She remained still, puzzled by the turmoil that held onto her.

God rest you merry gentlemen,
Let nothing you dismay.

The carolers tunes rang down the empty hall, offering a sinister ambiance to an already dreadful place. Marci looked down to where she had last seen the two men fighting, it was difficult to make out but it almost looked as though the floor contained a dark hole where they had last been.

Remember Christ our savior
Was born on Christmas day.

As the lights began to glow once more, it became abundantly clear that the two men were nowhere to be found. Only the carolers remained. They stood at the end of the hall looking like nothing more than dark shadows.

"Jacob?" She questioned. Her fingers slowly reached behind her, feeling the wall and hoping to find something to throw towards the unkempt shadows.

"Marci," Jacob whispered. She quickly turned, but just as fast as she could've reacted, she threw herself back and landed onto the floor. Standing in the doorway was the Itch Man. He held his hand out, and a bit of sand began to trickle to the floor.

"Only the guilty need fear me," he muttered.

"Its you?" Marci realized. "You're the Itch Man."

Chapter 9

Marci had never considered herself to be even remotely athletic, and yet tonight, she found herself soaring down the halls of a mental hospital with the grace and stamina of a true Olympian. She was barefoot and glad to be. After seeing the Itch Man, it was the first thing she knew to do. Escape was essential and it certainly wasn't going to happen in heels.

She reached a door that was labeled storage and came to a quick halt. Her heart was racing but she had to contain her breath, lest she give herself away. The Itch Man's steps were silent, not mute, but pretty darn close. In order to hear him, she'd have to be extra still.

"Where are you?" She whispered. His steps seemed faint. She opened the door as quietly as she could, stepped inside, and then pushed it close. Darkness surrounded her on all fronts, her only light was the bit that was coming in from the hallway. She slowly moved her arms forward, trying with the upmost urgency not to knock anything to the floor.

The dragging steps of her pursuer began to grow louder. He was near. As she covered her mouth, she found herself feeling quite friendly with fear. It seemed like an overzealous boy, unwilling to give her a moments peace. Her mind wandered as she listened to the steps. How was any of this possible? She hadn't really even had time to piece the puzzle out. After all, it was barely an hour ago that both her AND Jacob were being pursued by the strange creature. Now, it seemed, Jacob WAS the creature. The logistics boggled her mind and threatened to drive her to madness. Had she been conversing with a dead man all this time? Was Jacob still Jacob? So many questions with no clear answers.

With the steps fading once more, it became clear he was moving on, but the question was, was there any sense to trying to escape? Waiting could just as easily have been a viable option. So long as he didn't find her in here, all would be fine.

"Come on," she muttered to herself. "You can't stay locked in this closet all night.

Her mind pleaded with her to remain put, but her heart seemed content with liberation. After a few minutes of self-doubt and debate, she pulled the door open. The halls were brightly lit and from the distance she could hear the conversations of a dozen or so voices.

"Hello?" She called out. A buzzer loudly blared into the air.

"Mam what are you doing in here?" An elderly, thick built woman asked.

Marci turned and rubbed her eyes. Was she losing her mind?

"I'm lost. I can't find the exit," she softly replied.

"You're not supposed to be here," the nurse reiterated. "You're trespassing. Now come on, I best take you to the doctor, he might have some questions for you."

Marci stared blankly at the woman, then proceeded to follow her down the twisting halls. The hospital was alive and well again, the sun was shining brightly through the distant windows and commotion rang across the halls.

"I found someone," the nurse announced as she stepped into a wide open area. Standing there with a notepad and paper was Jacob. He looked professional, wearing glasses, a tie and a sharp dress shirt.

"Marci?" He questioned. "What are you doing out of your room?"

"I…..I was hiding from the Itch Man," she whispered.

Jacob shook his head and approached.

"Marci I've told you. You can't play games until after our session." He looked down to her arms and pointed at the clear sign of irritation.

"I see we need to cut your nails again." He nodded to the nurse, who groaned and approached with a pair of nail clippers.

"If you keep scratching at yourself, you're going to have to be restrained to your bed again," Jacob threatened.

"You're not a doctor," Marci accused. "You work at Ellis Island."

"No Marci. That was your brother. The one who became obsessed with the idea he had a skin disease."

"You're lying!" She bellowed. She threw herself down onto the floor in a fit of rage. Everything was dark once more. Standing over her, was the Itch Man. He looked to her with an accusatory stare, then sprinkled a bit of sand onto her. It dropped slowly and landed atop her legs, then he turned around and began to skulk away.

"Jacob get back here," she demanded. She climbed to her feet, but at that moment, a sharp tingle arrived.

"I'm itchy," she cried. Her hands reached down and began furiously scratching at various parts of her body.

"Marci?" A voice questioned from the darkness of the hall. Jacob arrived with Dr. Gordon, each of them holding a lantern in their hands. As Jacob took notice of Marci's incessant itching, he suddenly found himself feeling horribly confused.

"Why her?" He questioned. Dr. Gordon handed his lantern to Jacob, then promptly approached Marci. She looked to him with dread and continued to scratch at herself.

"It got her," Dr. Gordon noted. He wrapped his arms around her and restrained her hands as best he could.

"I thought you said it was after you."

Jacob stood watching her with confusion as she struggled to break free of the doctor's grip.

"Nurse," he called out.

A door flung open, bringing a bright light and heavy set woman hurrying towards them.

"We need to restrain her," Dr. Gordon ordered. The nurse nodded and reached into her pocket. She quickly withdrew a needle and pressed it into Marci's shoulder. The effect of the sedative was quite instant.

Marci toppled over with heavy breaths and vacant eyes.

"Another crazy one itching huh?" The nurse remarked. Dr. Gordon bowed his head and climbed to his feet.

"We got separated," Jacob explained.

He glanced Marci over and began to grow tearful.

"What will happen to her?"

Dr. Gordon shrugged and studied the unconscious woman.

"We'll keep her here. Keep her restrained so that she can't hurt herself. We have a few others that have come down with this."

He approached Jacob and gave his shoulder a firm squeeze.

"We'll keep her alive."

"But why her?" Jacob repeated. "Why her?"

"I think perhaps she would be able to answer that better than I," Dr. Gordon explained. They both looked down to her, feeling a bit of unease. The nearby nurse stood still, shaking her head as she glanced to the slumbering woman, then pursed her lips and reached towards her elbow giving it a subtle, but audible scratch. Dr. Gordon and Jacob looked up, sharing a nervous glance.

Silent night, holy night
All is calm, all is bright
Round yon virgin
Mother and child
Holy infant so tender and mild
Sleep in heavenly peace
Sleep in heavenly peace

The End

Since the initial outbreak of the compulsive itching disorder, sightings and reports of the Itch Man have increased at an alarming rate. Many have reported seeing him not long before being afflicted with the compulsive need to tame an unreachable scratch. Most of these sightings have been documented and reported to news outlets throughout the years. For more on these *so-called* sightings, stay tuned for the upcoming compiled works entitled *Chronicles of The Itch Man*.

Made in the USA
Middletown, DE
12 March 2018